Grandpa Green

LANE SMITH

Roaring Brook Press
New York

Published by Roaring Brook Press
Roaring Brook Press is a division of Holtzbrinck Publishing Holdings Limited Partnership
175 Fifth Avenue, New York, New York 10010
mackids.com

Library of Congress Cataloging-in-Publication Data
Smith, Lane.
    Grandpa Green / Lane Smith. — 1st ed.
        p.   cm.
    Summary: A child explores the ordinary life of his extraordinary great-grandfather,
as expressed in his topiary garden.
    ISBN 978-1-59643-607-7 (alk. paper)
    [1. Grandfathers—Fiction.   2. Gardens—Fiction.]   I. Title.
    PZ7.S6538Gr 2011
    [E]—dc22
                                                    2010038729

Roaring Brook Press books are available for special promotions and premiums.
For details contact: Director of Special Markets, Holtzbrinck Publishers.

The characters in this book were rendered with brush and waterproof drawing ink.
The foliage was created with watercolor, oil paint, and digital paint.

First edition 2011
Book design by Molly Leach
Printed in June 2011 in the United States of America by Worzalla, Stevens Point, Wisconsin

10 9 8 7 6 5 4 3 2

He was born a really long time ago,

before computers or cell phones or television.

He grew up on a farm with
pigs and corn and carrots . . .

and eggs.

In fourth grade
he got chicken pox.*

*Not from the chickens.

He had to stay home from school.
So he read stories about secret gardens
and wizards and a little engine that could.

In middle school

he stole his first kiss.

Heyworth Public Library

After high school his wish was to study horticulture,

but he went to a world war instead.

He met his future
wife in a little café.

When the war was over, they were married.

They had many happy years
together and never, ever fought.

At least to hear *him* tell it.

They had kids, way more grandkids, and a great-grandkid, me.

He used to remember everything.

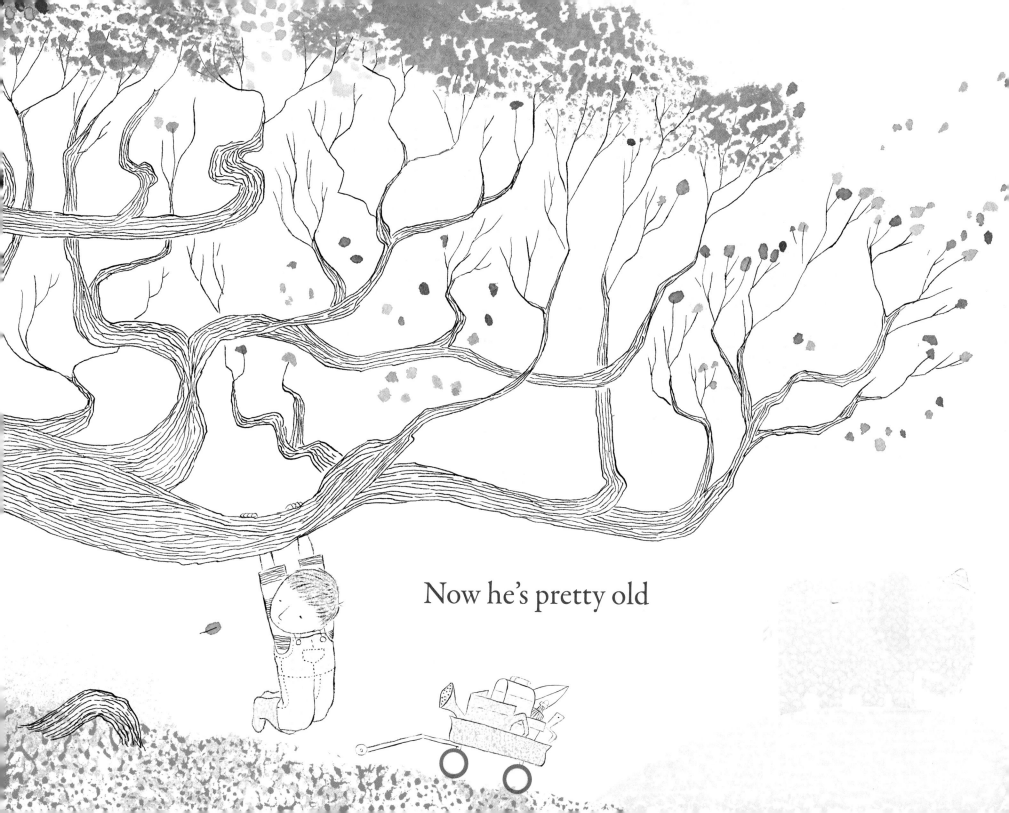

Now he's pretty old

and he sometimes forgets things

like his favorite floppy straw hat.

But the important stuff,

the garden remembers